SWEET VALLEY KIDS

LEFT-OUT ELIZABETH

Written by
Molly Mia Stewart

Created by
FRANCINE PASCAL

Illustrated by
Ying-Hwa Hu

D0028784

A BANTAM SKYLARK BOOK©
NEW YORK • TORONTO • LONDON • SYDNEY • AUCKLAND

RL 2, 005–008

LEFT-OUT ELIZABETH
A Bantam Skylark Book / January 1992

Sweet Valley High® and Sweet Valley Kids are
trademarks of Francine Pascal

Conceived by Francine Pascal
Produced by Daniel Weiss Associates, Inc.
33 West 17th Street
New York, NY 10011

Cover art by Susan Tang

Skylark Books is a registered trademark of Bantam Books, a
division of Bantam Doubleday Dell Publishing Group, Inc.
Registered in U.S. Patent and Trademark Office and elsewhere.

ISBN 0-553-15921-6

Published simultaneously in the United States and Canada

Bantam Books are published by Bantam Books, a division of Ban-
tam Doubleday Dell Publishing Group, Inc. Its trademark,
consisting of the words "Bantam Books" and the portrayal of a
rooster, is Registered in U.S. Patent and Trademark Office and in
other countries. Marca Registrada. Bantam Books, 666 Fifth Ave-
nue, New York, New York 10103.

PRINTED IN THE UNITED STATES OF AMERICA

OPM 0 9 8 7 6 5 4 3 2 1

To Aaron James Kowan

CHAPTER 1

Snow!

"When will we see some snow?" Elizabeth Wakefield asked impatiently, pressing her nose against the car window.

"I can't wait," said her twin sister, Jessica. "It's going to be so much fun. Snowmen, snow angels, snowball fights . . ."

Mr. Wakefield laughed. "Don't forget skiing! That's why we're going, isn't it?"

"You bet!" said Todd Wilkins, who was in second grade with the twins. He pointed out the window. "These are just foothills we're driving through now," he said knowledgeably. "The real mountains are much higher. That's where the snow is."

"Yeah, and the ski slopes," added Steven, the twins' older brother.

It was winter break, and the Wakefields and the Wilkinses were going on a four-day ski trip together. All the kids were riding with Mr. Wakefield, while Mrs. Wakefield and Todd's parents followed in the Wilkinses' car. Elizabeth had never seen snow, and she had never been skiing before, but she was sure she was going to love both. And the trip would be even more fun with Todd along. He was one of her best friends.

"I'm glad we could all go on this trip together," said Elizabeth, smiling at Todd. "You're going to teach me everything you know about skiing, right?" Todd had been skiing four times before.

2

Todd nodded. "Sure. You'll love it. It's even more fun than soccer."

Back home in Sweet Valley, Elizabeth enjoyed being outdoors, and she played all kinds of sports. She and Todd were on the same team in the Sweet Valley Soccer League.

Jessica didn't like to play soccer. She preferred playing inside with dolls, so that her clothes wouldn't get messy. But even though she didn't enjoy many sports, she was looking forward to trying skiing for the first time.

Although Jessica and Elizabeth were different from each other in many ways, they loved being twins. They shared almost everything, including their looks. Both girls had blue-green eyes, and long blond hair with bangs. When they dressed alike not even their best friends at Sweet Valley Elementary could tell them apart, except by looking at their name bracelets.

Elizabeth rolled down her window. "Brr! It's getting so cold! I can't believe we're still in California."

"That's because we're going up," Todd explained. "It gets colder the higher up you go."

The road was becoming steeper, and Jessica could see tall peaks rising up ahead of them. "Look!" she yelled suddenly. "Snow!"

"Where?" Elizabeth cried, leaning over her sister to see better.

Jessica pointed to a shadowy slope on the side of the road. Sure enough, there was a large patch of white snow. "Can we get out, Dad?" Steven asked.

"We'll be at the resort in just a few more minutes," Mr. Wakefield said, laughing. "Be patient. You'll have plenty of time to play in the snow."

Soon, they began to see signs for the ski area. Elizabeth was so excited she could hardly sit still. She couldn't wait to find out what snow felt like. As the car turned up a winding road, she saw wide ski slopes up ahead. There were poles and wires leading up the mountains. They looked almost like telephone poles, except that there were benches hanging from the wires.

"Those are the chair lifts," Todd said. "That's how skiers get to the tops of the slopes."

As the road curved again, a large ski lodge with a wooden deck came into view. To one side of the lodge was a group of smaller buildings, called chalets. The two families were going to share one of the chalets.

Mr. Wakefield parked the car. As the kids

jumped out, Mrs. Wakefield and Mr. and Mrs. Wilkins arrived in the other car.

"Isn't this great?" Jessica exclaimed, grabbing a handful of snow. "It's so cold!"

"And wet!" Elizabeth added with a giggle. She tossed a handful of snow at Steven.

"Missed me by a mile!" he boasted, making a face at Elizabeth.

"But I didn't!" Jessica shouted, sneaking up behind Steven and dumping an armful of snow over his head. She screamed and ran away as Steven started to make a huge snowball. "This one has your name on it, Jessica!" he warned her jokingly.

Elizabeth smiled as she watched them. She was having fun already.

Mrs. Wakefield stretched her arms and took a deep breath. "This mountain air smells wonderful. Why don't you kids take a

look at the slopes while we check in at the main desk. And try not to get each other *too* wet!"

Together, Jessica, Elizabeth, Todd, and Steven ran to watch the skiers.

"Look at how fast that guy is going!" Todd said. "He must be a real professional."

Elizabeth looked where Todd was pointing. A man in a bright green ski suit was speeding down the slope. He turned and stopped suddenly, sending up a spray of white powder from under his skis.

"I'll never be able to go that fast!" Elizabeth said.

Todd put his hands in his jacket pockets. "I bet I can," he said confidently. "It's a lot easier than it looks, once you get the hang of it."

Jessica pointed to a sign with an arrow on

it. "'This way to the bunny slope,'" she read. "That's where I'm skiing."

"Mom says we all have to start there," Elizabeth said. "We're all beginners."

"Well, *I'm* not really a beginner," Todd said quickly. "But I'll ski there with you, anyway."

Elizabeth didn't say anything. She knew Todd was showing off because he'd been skiing before, but she was too excited to care.

Jessica was watching two girls walk clumsily across the snow in their heavy ski boots.

"I hope I don't fall down," Jessica said. "It must be hard to get up again with those boots on."

"Don't worry," Elizabeth said. "You'll do great. Let's go find out when we can have our first ski lesson. I can't wait to get started!"

CHAPTER 2

The Bunny Slope

"Look," Jessica said, as they all went into the lobby of the lodge. "There's a ski shop. Let's go in."

The others followed her into the shop. Dozens of colorful ski parkas and jumpsuits crowded the tiny shop, and racks of ski equipment lined the wall behind the counter.

"I wish I could have one of these!" Jessica said, touching a bright pink ski suit. "We'll probably be the only ones wearing plain old jeans and winter jackets."

"Wow," Steven said. "Look!"

Jessica, Elizabeth, and Todd crowded

around him. He was standing in front of a glass case full of colorful ski goggles. "Those are totally cool," Todd said. "I wish I had a pair!"

"You already have goggles," Elizabeth said. "I saw them in the car."

"Yeah, but not like these," Todd said. "These are real, professional goggles. I can tell."

Elizabeth looked more closely at the goggles in the case. "Wow, I can tell, too, just by looking at the price! They cost fifty dollars a pair!"

"Well, I should save my money and get some. I'll need them on the tougher slopes," Todd said boastfully.

Jessica wanted a pair of the colorful goggles, too, even though she wasn't planning to try any difficult slopes on this trip. She knew her parents would never buy them for her, though, and she only had three dollars of her own money for souvenirs.

"Who cares about that stuff?" Elizabeth asked. She pointed to a sign that said "Equipment Rental." "Come on, let's go!"

"Can I rent pink boots?" Jessica asked the young man behind the equipment counter.

"Coming right up," the man said with a smile.

"I get the same kind of boots every time I ski," Todd said loudly.

"All *four* big times," Jessica whispered to Elizabeth.

By the time their parents found them a few minutes later, they were all fitted for boots, skis, bindings, and poles. The ski shop pro had led them outside and was showing them how to attach their boots to the bindings on the skis.

"While we were checking in at the front desk we signed you all up for your first ski lesson," Mr. Wilkins announced after the kids had practiced putting on their skis and taking them off again. "It starts in ten minutes."

"Let's go!" Elizabeth said eagerly. She grabbed her skis and poles and clumped toward the bunny slope in her ski boots.

A few minutes later, they joined a group of other kids at the bottom of the hill. A woman in red ski pants and a white sweater said hello to everyone.

"My name is Fran," she said. "We're going to start out slowly. I want you to stand on your skis and bend your knees."

"That sounds pretty easy," Jessica said to Elizabeth. She bent her knees, holding onto her ski poles for balance.

"Now, keep your knees bent and hold your poles up under your elbows," Fran continued.

The tips of Jessica's poles were stuck in the snow. She pulled them out and tucked them under her elbows. That made balancing harder, and when she moved one foot forward, her ski started sliding out in front of her.

"Oops!" she said, jabbing her poles back down to stop herself from sliding away.

"Just relax," Todd told her. "It's not really scary."

Fran smiled. "That's good advice. Now try pointing the tips of your skis together so they make a 'Vee.' That's called a snowplow. It will help you control your speed."

14

"I've skied before," Todd said, raising his hand. "Do I still have to do a snowplow?"

"Why don't you try it and we'll see how you do," Fran told him. "Now we're all going to go up the rope tow, and then we'll try coming down."

Jessica glanced at the rope tow. It was a thick rope that went around a pulley and up along one side of the short, gentle bunny slope. "How do you do it?" she asked, feeling nervous.

"Follow me," Fran said, pushing herself along with her poles.

The group followed her slowly. Jessica thought it felt strange to have long skis attached to her feet. She had trouble moving where she wanted to go, because her skis kept slipping around on top of the packed snow. Finally, she reached the rope tow. Fran was already there.

"Loop the straps of your poles over your wrists. Then grab the rope in both hands, and it will pull you right up," Fran explained. "Just make sure you keep both skis pointing straight ahead of you."

Todd sidestepped over to the rope tow. "It's simple," he called back. "Just watch." He bent his knees, grabbed the rope, and started sliding up the hill. When he got to the top, he let go. Then he turned around and waved to them. "Come on!"

Elizabeth and Steven quickly joined the line, but Jessica hung back. The rope tow looked fun, she thought, but it also looked kind of scary. Soon everyone had been towed up the slope except her and Fran.

"Ready to go?" Fran asked.

Jessica nodded and stepped up to the rope tow. "OK," she whispered. "Here I go."

The rope was running along next to her. She took a deep breath and grabbed it. "Whoa!" she cried as it tugged her up. Her skis wobbled a little but she straightened them out. In a flash, she was with the others. "That was fun!" she told Elizabeth breathlessly.

"Terrific," Fran said when she joined them a moment later. "Now, one at a time, put your skis in a snowplow, and start down. If you think you're going too fast, just sit down on your skis."

"I'll go first," Elizabeth said.

Jessica watched as her sister pushed off and skied slowly toward the bottom of the hill. Elizabeth made it look so simple.

"OK," Jessica said, taking a deep breath.

"I'm next!" She pointed the tips of her skis together and pushed off with her poles. Suddenly she was skiing!

"Wow!" Jessica shouted, breaking into a smile. "This is fun!"

The bunny slope wasn't steep, and it leveled off at the bottom. In just a moment, Jessica glided to a careful stop beside Elizabeth.

"Isn't this great?" Elizabeth asked. "I want to go skiing every year."

"So do I," Jessica said, scooting along toward the rope tow. "Let's ski down again!"

CHAPTER 3

Show-off

After a good night's sleep and a hearty breakfast at the lodge, Elizabeth, Jessica, Todd, and Steven were ready to hit the slopes again.

"The resort is having a snow sculpture contest," Mr. Wakefield told them as they were all getting ready to go outside. "There will be prizes in different age categories."

"Great!" Steven said. "We'll make something really cool."

"Is that a joke?" Elizabeth asked with a smile. "Snow? Cool?" Everybody laughed.

"Have fun, kids," Mrs. Wakefield said, as

she put on her skis. "You can ski the beginner slopes all morning if you want."

Elizabeth looked at the almost empty ski slopes. The sunlight on the snow was blindingly bright, but it made everything look very pretty. "Let's hurry up before it gets crowded," she said.

"I'm going to ski some of the harder trails today," Todd announced. "The beginner slope is too easy for me."

Mr. Wilkins shook his head. "Stick with the others, young man."

"Liz is already just as good a skier as you are," Jessica told Todd.

Elizabeth smiled. "Thanks, Jess, you're a good skier, too."

After their parents left for the chair lift, the kids finished getting ready. Elizabeth had long underwear on under her jeans and turtleneck, but the sunshine was warm. As she picked up her ski poles, she saw a boy about Steven's age coming toward them.

"Hi," he said with a friendly smile. "Did you just get here?"

"We came yesterday," Steven said. "We're staying four days."

"My name is Mark," the boy said. "I come here with my parents every year. Have you all been skiing before?"

Todd pushed himself forward on his skis. "I have, but it's *their* first time. I'm Todd."

Mark had a pair of bright orange goggles up on his forehead. They looked just like the ones in the ski shop. He was wearing purple ski pants and a matching jacket, and his skis were black with purple and orange streaks. "Isn't skiing the greatest?" he asked.

"I think it's—" Elizabeth began.

"Totally cool," Todd interrupted her. "I like all sports, but skiing is the best. Schussing down the slope is awesome."

"What's schussing?" Jessica asked.

Todd rolled his eyes. "It's another word for skiing."

"Why didn't you just say skiing?" Jessica asked him.

Elizabeth guessed that Todd was trying to let Mark know he wasn't a beginner. She wished that Todd wouldn't show off so much. Usually he didn't boast at all.

"There are lots of special ski terms, Jessica," Steven said in his most mature voice. "You'll learn."

Mark nodded at Todd. "I love sports, too. I'm in Little League, and I also play football and street hockey."

"Todd and I are both in the Sweet Valley Soccer League," Elizabeth began. "I play—"

"We're undefeated so far," Todd interrupted again. "We'll probably win the city championship."

Mark adjusted his goggles over his eyes. They made him look like a professional skier. "That's cool," he said. "I wish my town had a soccer league. I'd join for sure."

"How long are you staying, Mark?" Steven asked.

By this time, Todd and Steven were standing with their backs to Elizabeth and Jessica. Elizabeth guessed that both boys wanted to make a good impression on Mark, because he was a good skier. But she didn't know why they had to ignore Jessica and her to do it.

Elizabeth stared at the back of Todd's

jacket. She and Todd were supposed to be good friends, but at the moment Todd was acting as though he had never seen her before in his life. Elizabeth didn't understand it at all.

CHAPTER 4

Left Out

"Come on," Jessica said. "Why are we standing around? Let's ski!"

"Can I ski with you guys?" Mark asked.

Todd and Steven both smiled. "Sure," Steven said.

"What level of trails do you ski?" Todd asked Mark.

"Mostly intermediate," Mark said. "How about you?"

Jessica broke in before Todd could start bragging about his skiing ability. "We're *all* skiing the beginner trails," she said. Todd looked embarrassed.

Mark shrugged. "That's all right. I'll go down the beginner trails with you. It's more fun than skiing alone."

They shuffled over to the chair lift. Cars that looked like seats from a Ferris wheel came down the mountain on a cable, turned around inside a building, and scooped up three people before starting back up the mountain again. Jessica thought it looked like a lot more fun than the rope tow. Her arms and shoulders were still aching from holding on the day before.

"I'll ride with Jessica and Todd," Elizabeth said.

Todd pointed at Steven and Mark. "I'm riding with them," he said.

"Oh." Elizabeth looked disappointed. "But you'll still ski with me like you promised, right?"

28

"Sure," Todd replied quickly, not looking at her. Then he slid forward to talk to Mark and Steven.

Jessica could tell her sister was unhappy because Todd was ignoring her. "Todd's acting like a real show-off," she said to Elizabeth. "Just pretend you don't know him— or Steven either."

"He's supposed to be my friend," Elizabeth mumbled.

Jessica didn't know what to say. She hated to see her twin look so upset.

Soon, the boys reached the front of the line. They moved into place and waited for the chair lift to come and scoop them up. When it did, they hopped on and lowered the safety bar in front of them.

"Now us," Elizabeth said.

Jessica stood next to Elizabeth and

watched over her shoulder. A chair came swooping around toward them. Jessica fell back into it and felt it lift her up until they were moving along high above the snowy slope.

"Weeeeeh! This is like a ride at the amusement park!" she said. She looked down at the ground below. "Isn't it fun?"

Elizabeth didn't answer. She was looking at the chair ahead of them. The three boys were waving their arms and shouting and laughing.

"Isn't this fun?" Jessica asked louder.

"I guess so," Elizabeth said slowly.

For the rest of the ride, they watched the skiers speeding down the slopes underneath them.

"I wish you could just ride the chair lift up and down all day," Jessica said, as they hopped off at the top and joined the boys. "That's my kind of sport."

Steven heard her. "Girls," he said, shaking his head.

Jessica ignored him. She looked around. Several trails started nearby. They were labeled with names like "Rolling Along," "Captain's Folly," and "Do-Si-Do."

"Do-Si-Do is a good trail," Mark said. "It's fun but easy."

"OK, let's go for it," Todd said, shoving off quickly.

Elizabeth began to follow him, but Jessica stopped her. "Liz? Will you wait for me?"

The boys kept on going. Elizabeth looked disappointed that they had left her behind. But she smiled at Jessica. "I'll ski with you. Who needs them, anyway?"

The two of them skied down the Do-Si-Do

trail very slowly. Every time Jessica felt herself going too fast, she sat down on her skis.

When they reached the bottom, Elizabeth could see that the boys were already almost at the front of the lift line. Todd and Steven were too busy talking to Mark to even notice when the twins joined the line. Elizabeth stared sadly at Todd's back. She just wanted Todd to be her friend again.

CHAPTER 5

Five Is a Crowd

"So, how do you like skiing?" Mrs. Wakefield asked that evening at dinner.

"I love it," Elizabeth said, spearing some peas with her fork.

Their table in the lodge dining room was near a large fireplace with a roaring log fire. It made the whole room cozy and warm.

"I like it, too," Jessica said. "But I'm really tired."

"We met this guy named Mark," Steven said. "He's my age. And he's a really good skier."

"Right," Todd added. "He gave us lots of tips, but I think I'm already almost as good as he is."

"He sounds nice," Mr. Wilkins said with a smile.

Elizabeth chewed her peas slowly. She was tired of hearing about how terrific Mark was. All day long, Todd and Steven had been bragging and showing off to impress their new friend. And all day long, Todd had made excuses for not skiing with Elizabeth.

"He's OK," Jessica said, frowning at Todd. "But I think Liz skis as well as any of you."

"Elizabeth has always been a good athlete," Mrs. Wilkins said.

Steven shook his head. "Not like Mark. He's on all his school teams, and he goes to baseball camp in the summers. Dad, can I go to baseball camp next summer, too?

Maybe I could even go to the same one as Mark."

"We'll see," Mr. Wakefield said.

Elizabeth stared down at her plate. If she heard one more word about Mark, she thought she would scream.

"Have you kids decided what kind of snow sculpture you're going to make?" Mrs. Wakefield asked as she buttered a roll.

Elizabeth cheered up at the thought of the contest. "How about a dragon?" she said. "Or a turtle."

"Or a spaceship!" Steven suggested.

"That's a good idea. We could even make aliens," Elizabeth said.

Todd smiled at her. "A spaceship would be excellent!"

Elizabeth smiled back. She was glad that Todd was being friendly again.

"We can start tomorrow," Jessica said. "My muscles are so sore that I don't think I can go skiing all day again anyway."

"If everybody's finished eating, let's all have hot cocoa in front of the fire," Mrs. Wakefield suggested. "There's a big collection of board games by the door. Maybe you kids can find one to play."

"Good idea, Mom," Elizabeth said.

Everyone pulled comfortable chairs up close to the fireplace. Jessica went to the bookcase where the board games were kept. "How about Scrabble?" she said, pulling it off the shelf. "We can play as teams."

"I get to be on Elizabeth's team!" Todd said. "She never loses."

"OK," Elizabeth said happily. She looked at Jessica. "Sorry, but it looks like you're stuck with Steven."

Steven stuck out his tongue at her, and everyone laughed. Elizabeth felt much happier than she had all day. She knew Todd wanted to be on her team because they were friends, not just because she was a good Scrabble player.

They started to play. After a few minutes, Elizabeth and Todd were winning by ten points. "We're going to be the Scrabble champions of the lodge, right Elizabeth?" Todd said.

Steven took a sip of his cocoa. Then he put his cup down quickly. "Hey, there's Mark," he said.

"Where?" Todd asked, turning around. "Let's go see what he's doing."

Both boys stood up.

"Hey," Jessica complained. "Don't you want to finish the game?"

"You two can go ahead and play without us," Steven said, beginning to walk away.

Elizabeth looked up at Todd with a hurt expression on her face. "But I thought we were a team," she said softly.

"I'm going to go talk to Mark," Todd said. "You don't really need me." He hurried off after Steven.

Elizabeth sat back in her chair and crossed her arms. She didn't feel like playing anymore.

CHAPTER 6

The Snow Bunnies

In the morning, Jessica put on her long underwear, a pair of wool knee socks, a pink turtleneck, a pink sweater, jeans, and her snow boots.

"Come on!" she called to her sister. "Let's go wake up Todd and Steven for breakfast. Then we can start our snow sculpture."

After a large breakfast of pancakes, bacon, orange juice, and cocoa, Jessica led the way outside. There was a large, flat yard behind the lodge, where several snow sculptures had already been finished.

"Let's take a vote," Elizabeth said. "Who wants to build a spaceship?"

Steven and Todd raised their hands.

"Who wants to make a snow dragon?" Elizabeth asked.

Jessica and Elizabeth raised their hands. Then Todd raised his hand.

"You can't vote twice," Steven said.

"I changed my mind," Todd explained.

Elizabeth looked happy that Todd had voted for her idea. She put on her mittens.

"Let's make some big snowballs for the body," Jessica suggested. She scooped up some snow and packed it in her hands.

Todd and Steven started rolling some big snowballs. With each step that they took, the snow made crunching sounds under their feet.

"I didn't know snow could be so noisy," Elizabeth said with a laugh. She was drawing an outline in the snow. "Let's give the dragon a long, spiky tail."

"And big spikes on its back," Todd said.

Jessica's mittens were getting wet, but she didn't really mind. She had always wanted to play in the snow, but since it never snowed in Sweet Valley, this was her first chance.

"Hi," came a friendly voice.

Jessica turned around. Mark was walking toward them with a big smile on his face. "Uh-oh," she whispered.

She looked over at her sister. Elizabeth was staring at the ground and not saying anything.

"Hi, Mark," Steven called out.

Todd waved and dropped the snowball he was holding.

"What are you making?" Mark asked.

"Just a dumb dragon," Todd said. "It was Elizabeth's idea."

"You voted for it!" Jessica reminded him. She was angry at Todd. She knew he had promised to ski with Elizabeth and to help with the snow sculpture. But he kept forgetting his promises whenever Mark showed up.

"Are you skiing today?" Mark asked.

"Sure," Steven said quickly. "We were just helping the girls get started. We don't have to stay."

"But we were going to do this together," Elizabeth reminded him.

Todd shook his head. "You and Jessica can do it. We're going to ski. That's why we came on this trip."

"We don't have to ski every single minute,"

Jessica said. "Besides, my legs are tired, and I don't want to ski."

"You don't have to," Steven said. "We'll see you later."

Steven and Todd walked away with Mark. "We'll show them," Jessica said angrily. "We'll make something really great and win first prize. We're better off without them."

Elizabeth was packing some snow into a ball. She looked disappointed. "We won't be able to finish the dragon without their help," she said sadly. "It's too big."

"Let's make something else, then," Jessica said. She wanted to cheer up her sister. "I know! Let's make twins."

"Snow twins?" Elizabeth asked, beginning to smile.

"Sure. Twin bunnies for the bunny slope."

Elizabeth laughed. "A Jessica bunny and an Elizabeth bunny."

"Right," Jessica said. "We don't need Todd and Steven to have fun!"

CHAPTER 7

The Icy Slope

Elizabeth patted the large ears of her snow bunny. "Perfect," she said proudly.

The twin bunnies were almost as tall as Elizabeth and Jessica. They had snowball tails and tall, pointed ears.

"I'm crossing my fingers inside my mittens," Jessica said. "I hope we win a prize."

Elizabeth looked up at the ski trails. Making the snow sculptures had been fun, but she was eager to ski again. Nearby, several kids were sledding down a gentle hill.

"Let's get our skis on," Elizabeth said.

Jessica shook her head. "My legs still

ache. I think I'll go sledding instead. Do you want to come?"

Elizabeth thought about it. She was still upset at how Todd had acted earlier, but she really wanted to ski.

"No, you go ahead," she said. "I'll catch up with Todd and Steven."

A few minutes later Elizabeth found Todd, Steven, and Mark at the end of the lift line.

"Hi," Elizabeth said. "How many times have you gone up?"

"Tons," Todd said. "The conditions are a little icy."

Elizabeth knew he was showing off again by talking about "conditions." But she didn't say anything. Soon they reached the head of the line. "Who can I ride with?" she asked.

"I'm riding with Mark," Steven said quickly.

"I'll ride with you," Todd mumbled.

"We'll see you at the top," Mark called back, as he and Steven were carried away by the lift.

Elizabeth turned to Todd. "Why are you being so mean?" she blurted out. "We're supposed to be having fun *together.*"

"I'm not being mean," Todd said. They waited for the chair to pick them up, and then they lowered the safety bar.

"You promised to ski with me," Elizabeth said. "But you're always going off with Steven and Mark."

"I'm skiing with you now, aren't I?" Todd said grumpily as they rose higher into the air.

Elizabeth stared at him, but he pretended

not to notice. They didn't say anything else until they reached the top.

"Let's try one of the intermediate trails," Steven suggested when they were all together. "I'm tired of the beginner stuff."

"Yeah," Todd said. "I want to try a harder slope before we leave."

Mark looked worried. "It's pretty icy today."

"We're supposed to stick to the beginner trails," Elizabeth added nervously.

Todd laughed. "I'm not a beginner."

"And I'm older than you," Steven added. "I'm definitely ready for the intermediate slopes."

"I'm not," Elizabeth said. "I'm not skiing down those trails."

"I thought you wanted to ski with us," Todd said. "And now you won't."

50

Elizabeth was so angry that she gritted her teeth and headed for the beginner trail without answering.

"Come on," Todd said to Mark and Steven. "Let's hit the slope."

The trail Elizabeth was going to ski went down the mountain beside the more difficult trail. The trails were separated by a line of dark green fir trees, but Elizabeth could see enough through the trees to tell that the intermediate slope was much steeper than hers. She could hear the boys' excited voices as they started down the hill.

Elizabeth decided to forget about the way Todd was acting and have a good time anyway. The slope was a little bit icy in spots, and that made skiing slightly tricky. But she skied slowly and carefully. It was fun, and the snow-covered trees looked like something out of a fairy tale. Then suddenly she heard a cry for help from the other side of the trees.

"Whoa!" yelled Steven. "Slow down!"

"Sit down on your skis," Mark shouted.

Elizabeth knew it was Todd who was in trouble.

Then she heard him shout out in fear. "I can't stop!"

CHAPTER 8

Wipeout!

Jessica climbed back up the sledding hill and looked toward the beginner ski trail. It made a gentle curve down the mountain. Many skiers were gliding down. Jessica recognized Elizabeth among them. She waved and sledded down to meet her.

"Hi!" Jessica called out as she ran over to the bottom of the ski slope.

Elizabeth didn't answer right away. She was staring back up the mountain, looking very nervous.

"What's wrong?" Jessica asked.

"It's Todd," Elizabeth explained, putting

one hand up to shield her eyes from the sun as she searched the slope. "Do you see the boys anywhere?"

Jessica squinted to see in the bright sunlight. One of the trails made a long zigzag back and forth across the side of the mountain, with some long, steep drops in it. Halfway up, Jessica spotted Todd, Steven, and Mark. They had stopped.

"There they are. Why did they stop?" she asked, beginning to feel worried.

"I could hear them at the top," Elizabeth said. "The trail they're on is longer than the beginner one that I took, and it's icy. I think they stopped because it's too hard to ski. I could hear them yelling about how fast they were going. I hope they take off their skis and walk the rest of the way down."

Jessica bit her lip. "Do you think they will?"

The moment she asked the question, she saw Todd, Steven, and Mark push off and start skiing down. Almost at once, all three boys picked up speed.

"They're going too fast!" Jessica said. Her heart was pounding loudly in her chest. Her brother skimmed down the mountainside, nearly hitting some other skiers. Even from where they were standing, the twins could tell he was out of control.

"Look out!" Elizabeth yelled, sounding frightened.

As they watched, Steven waved his arms wildly and fell. Snow sprayed up all around as he tumbled down the rest of the slope. Jessica screamed and started running.

"Somebody call the first-aid patrol!" a man standing nearby shouted.

Everyone was running toward Steven.

Soon he was surrounded by a crowd. "Oh, ow!" he moaned.

"What hurts?" Elizabeth asked as she reached his side.

"Everything!" Steven said. His skis had come off and slid away. He was holding his knee with both hands.

"Here comes the ski patrol," a woman announced. Steven was put on a special ski stretcher, bundled in blankets, and whisked away.

Jessica glanced up the slope. Mark was skiing down without any problem. But Todd had taken off his skis and was walking down the rest of the trail. He looked very shaken up.

"Is Steven OK?" he asked as he and Mark finally joined the twins.

"I think he hurt his knee," Elizabeth said.

"We have to find Mom and Dad," Jessica whispered, feeling tears come to her eyes.

"Uh-oh," Todd said with a gulp. His face was very pale. "Wait until my mom and dad find out I went on the intermediate trail. I'm going to be in big trouble."

CHAPTER 9

Poor Steven

For the rest of the afternoon Elizabeth and Jessica stayed in the lodge and waited for news from their parents, who were with Steven at the hospital. Todd's parents had grounded him for disobeying the rule about staying on the beginner trails. He had to stay alone in their chalet until dinner.

"Here's some nice hot cocoa for you girls," a waitress said, putting down a tray by their chairs. "It's a house rule. When your brother gets hurt, you get free cocoa."

"Thanks," Elizabeth said with a worried smile.

Jessica sipped her cocoa and looked at the fire. "I hope his leg isn't broken."

"Me, too," Elizabeth said. She heard someone come into the room. When she looked up, she saw that it was Mark.

"Hi," Mark said. "I'm sorry about what happened. Is Steven OK?"

"We don't know yet," Jessica muttered.

"I tried to tell them that the slopes were too icy," Mark explained. "I had a hard time coming down the trail myself."

Elizabeth could tell that Mark was honestly sorry about Steven, and she knew it wasn't his fault that Todd and Steven had tried to impress him. "Do you want to play cards with us?" she asked.

"Sure," Mark said, smiling. "Where's Todd?"

Jessica drew a finger across her throat.

"He's grounded. He was only supposed to ski on the beginner trails."

"Oh, what a bummer," said Mark. "What do you want to play?"

"How about go-fish," Jessica suggested.

"That's my favorite," Mark said eagerly. "Who wants to shuffle first?"

Just before dinner time, Mr. and Mrs. Wakefield returned with Steven.

"What happened?" Jessica asked when she saw her brother hobbling into the lodge on crutches. "Is your leg broken?"

"He sprained his knee," Mrs. Wakefield said. "He has to stay off it for a few weeks."

Steven looked pale and tired. "That'll teach me to try skiing on the hard trails before I'm ready," he said with a smile.

"You were doing OK until you fell," Elizabeth said.

Mr. Wakefield pulled a large, cozy chair close to the fireplace. Steven walked over with his crutches, sat down, and propped his injured leg on another chair.

Just then, Todd walked in with his parents. He had his hands in his pockets and an embarrassed look on his face.

"Hi," he mumbled to Steven. "How's your knee?"

"It's just a sprain," Steven said.

Todd nodded. "I hope it doesn't hurt too much." He looked at Elizabeth. "You were right. We should all have stayed on the easy trails. Sorry."

"That's OK," Elizabeth told him.

"Can I ski with you tomorrow?" Todd asked.

Elizabeth looked at Mr. and Mrs. Wilkins. "Is Todd grounded tomorrow, too?" she asked.

"Well, I don't think Todd will make the same mistake again," Mr. Wilkins said. "So, since it's the last day, he can ski."

Elizabeth and Todd smiled at each other.

"Listen, kids. They're judging the snow sculptures tomorrow," Mrs. Wilkins said. "How did your spaceship turn out?"

Everyone was silent for a moment. The boys were embarrassed to admit they hadn't helped. Jessica pointed to the window. "Look out there, and see if you can guess which one Liz and I did."

The adults went to the window. Outside, bright lamps lit up the sculpture area. Snowmen and dragons and castles shone in the light.

"I don't see—" Mrs. Wakefield began. "Oh! The bunnies!"

"They're twins," Elizabeth explained proudly.

"They look terrific," Mr. Wakefield said. "It must have been a lot of work."

Jessica crossed her fingers and looked at Elizabeth. "I hope we win the contest!"

CHAPTER 10

First Prize

When Jessica opened her eyes the next morning, she felt excited—and then disappointed. It was the last day of their ski trip.

"Do you think they picked the contest winners yet?" she asked on the way to breakfast at the lodge. She hopped up and down impatiently. They had to walk slowly so that Steven could keep up on his crutches.

"The list should be up on the bulletin board by now," Mrs. Wilkins said.

Jessica ran up the wooden steps to the lodge entrance. The bulletin board was inside the door. "I can't see!" she said. "The list is up too high."

"They've got the winners listed here," Mr. Wakefield said, reading the typed notice. "Hmm . . . age six to eight category. Third place, snow car. I thought that was pretty good. But I wonder what kind of gas mileage it gets."

"Come on, Dad!" Elizabeth laughed impatiently.

Jessica danced from one foot to the other. "Did we win?"

"Second place," Mr. Wakefield continued slowly. "The snow turtle. It looked more like a snow apple pie to me."

"Dad!" Jessica exclaimed.

"Ned, stop teasing. They're frantic," Mrs. Wilkins said. "Girls, it says first place goes to the twin snow bunnies!"

Jessica let out a shriek and hugged Elizabeth. "We won! We won!"

Steven was reading the notice. "Hey! You know what your prize is? Those great ski goggles we saw in the ski shop."

"Really?" Jessica gasped. "I can't believe it."

Hand in hand, Jessica and Elizabeth ran into the shop. "We won some ski goggles!" Jessica announced to the cashier.

He smiled. "I guess you made those twin bunnies. They're pretty awesome."

Jessica watched excitedly while the man opened the case. "Can we pick the color we want?" she asked.

"Of course," he said cheerfully.

When Jessica and Elizabeth joined the others at breakfast, they were both wearing their new goggles. Jessica's were yellow, and Elizabeth's were light blue.

"Those are so cool," Steven said enviously.

"I wish I had a pair," Todd added.

Mrs. Wakefield gave the kids a warm smile. "So, aside from Steven's accident, did you all have fun on this trip?"

Elizabeth nodded. "I love skiing," she said. "I want to come back every year."

"Do you think you'll ever give it another try, Steven?" Mrs. Wilkins asked.

"Absolutely," Steven answered. "But I'll stick to the easy trails until I'm a better skier."

"Good thinking," Mr. Wakefield said, ruffling Steven's hair. "If the rest of you hurry, you can get in a few good runs before we have to pack up and leave."

"Come on!" Jessica said. She was eager to ski again now that she was rested up from the day before. She was also eager to show off her new goggles.

While Steven watched from the deck, Elizabeth, Jessica, and Todd spend the morning skiing the beginner trails. All too soon, they saw their parents waving to them from the lodge.

"It's time to go!" Mr. Wakefield shouted.

After they returned their ski equipment, they had a quick lunch. Mark came over as they were leaving the lodge.

"Bye," he said. "Maybe I'll see you all next year."

"I hope so," Todd answered. "We can have a great time skiing together."

"And next time, maybe you could help us

build another prize-winning snow sculpture," Elizabeth added, smiling at Mark.

"That would be great," Mark replied.

Outside, the adults were still trying to cram the last few pieces of luggage into the cars.

"Let's make snow angels," Elizabeth suggested.

"I can't," Steven answered as he hobbled to the car.

"I don't want to get any more snow down my back," Jessica said. "I had enough of that while we were skiing."

Todd looked at Elizabeth and smiled. "I'll make angels with you," he said.

At the count of three, Elizabeth and Todd both fell over backwards in the deep snow and moved their arms and legs back and forth. Elizabeth giggled as she felt snow go into her ear.

"Don't forget the halo," Todd reminded her. He got up to draw one with his fingers.

Elizabeth nodded. She was glad that she and Todd were still special friends.

On the way home, a song about Hawaii came on the car radio. "Grandma and Grandpa are going there on vacation," Mr. Wakefield told the twins. "They'll be gone for most of February."

"February?" Elizabeth said. "Does that mean they won't be able to come visit us for Valentine's Day this year?"

"I'm afraid not," Mr. Wakefield replied. "But I'm sure they'll send something nice from Hawaii."

"Wow!" Jessica said, sitting back in the

seat. "A Valentine's present from Hawaii. I wonder what it'll be?"

Will Jessica and Elizabeth get the same present? Find out in Sweet Valley Kids #26, JESSICA'S SNOBBY CLUB.